Oswald's Camping Trip

by Dan Yaccarino
based on the teleplay by Suzanne Collins
illustrated by Jennifer Oxley

Simon Spotlight/Nick Jr.
New York   London   Toronto   Sydney   Singapore

Based on the
TV series *Oswald*®
as seen on Nick Jr.®

SIMON SPOTLIGHT
An imprint of Simon & Schuster Children's Publishing Division
1230 Avenue of the Americas, New York, New York 10020
Copyright © 2003 HIT Entertainment and
Viacom International Inc.
All rights reserved. NICKELODEON, NICK JR., *Oswald*, and all related
titles, logos, and characters are trademarks
of Viacom International Inc.
All rights reserved, including the right of
reproduction in whole or in part in any form.
SIMON SPOTLIGHT and colophon are
registered trademarks of Simon & Schuster.
Manufactured in the United States of America
First Edition
2 4 6 8 10 9 7 5 3 1
ISBN 0-689-85432-3

Oswald the octopus and his pet hot dog, Weenie, were getting ready for their camping trip with Daisy and Henry.

"Let's go!" said Oswald.

"Hup, two. Hup, two—we are campers through and through."

Henry said he thought it looked like
rain and they should stay home.
"It's not going to rain!" said Oswald.

Just in case, Henry packed
a few extra things.

"Hup, two, three, four—let's go wait outside the door."

"Hey there, camperoonies!" shouted Daisy. "Ready for the best camping trip ever?"

Henry said he thought it looked like rain and they should stay home.

"It's not going to rain!" said Oswald and Daisy.

"Hup, two. Hup, two—camping's what we like to do."

Henry stopped. "How about here?"
Oswald and Daisy wanted to camp a little farther away from the sidewalk.
"If it rains," said Henry, "we could get home in a hurry."

"It's not going to rain!" said Oswald and Daisy.

"Hup, two. Hup, two—let's go somewhere that's brand new!"

Soon they found
the perfect spot.

"Don't you think it looks like rain?" asked Henry.

Oswald and Daisy pitched the tent,
and Henry took a rest.

Then suddenly Oswald felt
something drip on his head.
"Uh-oh," said Oswald. "I think
it's starting to rain."

"Rain!" shouted Henry. "Aha! I knew this stuff would come in handy!"
But all of Henry's things blew away in the wind.

It was really starting to pour!

Oswald had an idea.

"Quick! Everyone under here!" called Oswald.

"Hup, two, three, four—
let's go home, it's gonna pour."

They finally made it home.

Henry said he knew it looked like rain
and they should have stayed home.

"Now the best camping trip ever is ruined!" said Daisy.

But Oswald had an idea.

"We could camp right here in the living room!" he said.

Henry told Oswald that you can't camp indoors. That would just be silly.

Daisy and Weenie thought it was a great idea.

They pitched the tent.

They sang songs, told
ghost stories, and had a snack.

It was the best camping trip ever.